W9-AUJ-672

FAIRLEE SCHOOL
WAS ALL I'D HOPED FOR . . .

"Our own TV, our own refrigerator, our own bathroom," I said. "Pretty neat."

"Yes, those are pleasant amenities," said Goober. "But physical conveniences are just a minor consideration. The important thing, of course, is the quality of instruction. After all, we are here to learn."

The most important thing for me to learn was how to live in the same room with Goober without wringing his neck. Or, if I *did* wring it, learn how to dispose of the body.

BANANA BLITZ

"Lightweight, breezy story . . . follow-up to Heide's funny *Banana Twist*."

—*Booklist*

"Hilarious . . . A story that snaps and crackles with kid-sized wit."

—*Kirkus Reviews*

Bantam Skylark Books of Related Interest
Ask your bookseller for the books you have missed

ARTHUR THE KID by Alan Coren
BANANA TWIST by Florence Parry Heide
BE A PERFECT PERSON IN JUST THREE
   DAYS! by Stephen Manes
BONES ON BLACK SPRUCE MOUNTAIN by
   David Budbill
THE CHOCOLATE TOUCH by Patrick Skene
   Catling
C.L.U.T.Z. by Marilyn Z. Wilkes
DANNY THE CHAMPION OF THE WORLD
   by Roald Dahl
ENCYCLOPEDIA BROWN'S BOOK OF
   WACKY CARS by Donald J. Sobol
NUTTY FOR PRESIDENT by Dean Hughes
OWLS IN THE FAMILY by Farley Mowat
SNOWSHOE TREK TO OTTER RIVER by
   David Budbill

FLORENCE PARRY HEIDE

Banana Blitz

A BANTAM SKYLARK BOOK®
TORONTO • NEW YORK • LONDON • SYDNEY • AUCKLAND

With love to the Wilson Connection, from Little Florence

T 1138

*This low-priced Bantam Book
has been completely reset in a type face
designed for easy reading, and was printed
from new plates. It contains the complete
text of the original hard-cover edition.*
NOT ONE WORD HAS BEEN OMITTED.

RL 6, 008–012

BANANA BLITZ
*A Bantam Book / published by arrangement with
Holiday House Inc.*

PRINTING HISTORY
Holiday House edition published March 1983
Bantam Skylark edition / June 1984

*Skylark Books is a registered trademark of Bantam Books, Inc.
Registered in U.S. Patent and Trademark Office and elsewhere.*

All rights reserved.
Copyright © 1983 by Florence Parry Heide.
Cover art copyright © 1984 by Bob Chronister.
*This book may not be reproduced in whole or in part, by
mimeograph or any other means, without permission.
For information address: Holiday House Inc.,
18 East 53rd Street, New York, N.Y. 10022.*

ISBN 0-553-15258-0

Published simultaneously in the United States and Canada

*Bantam Books are published by Bantam Books, Inc. Its trade-
mark, consisting of the words "Bantam Books" and the por-
trayal of a rooster, is Registered in U.S. Patent and Trademark
Office and in other countries. Marca Registrada. Bantam
Books, Inc., 666 Fifth Avenue, New York, New York 10103.*

PRINTED IN THE UNITED STATES OF AMERICA

O   0 9 8 7 6 5

Contents

1 · Maybe He'd Been Eaten by a Shark

All the way over to Fairlee School, I was congratulating myself on my cleverness at being admitted to the school. I kept making mental lists of all the advantages and disadvantages of leaving home. The pluses and the minuses, the good points and the bad. Dad and Mom were in the front seat and I was in the back. The closer we got to Fairlee, the longer my list of pluses got.

Sure, I love my parents, but they're still going through this phase of thinking I'm too young to make my own decisions. About anything. I guess this is what usually happens to parents. When you're born they *have* to do your thinking for you because you can't do too much of that yourself, and then they get into the habit. They keep trying to think for you practically all your *life*.

So it was going to be good to get away.

"Jonah, you're not eating a second candy bar, are you?" That was Mom. She had eyes in the back of her head.

"Nope," I said honestly. Actually, it was my third, not my second. I rarely lie outright to my parents. It's all in the way you say things.

I'd used up the last of my allowance to buy a supply of candy bars and stuff like that to keep in the refrigerator that I knew was going to be in my room at Fairlee. I'd saved out just enough for the ice cream I'd buy when I got there. Dad had given me a ten-dollar bill for school supplies, and that would keep me in junk food for a while, at least until he sent some more money.

"Most schools have very starchy diets, I'm afraid," Mom went on. "Don't have more than one helping of anything. And skip desserts, Jonah. Now that we're not going to be with you to help you to eat properly, you'll have to develop some strong health habits of your own."

"Yeah," I said. My parents helping me with

my diet meant that there was never anything in our apartment that anyone would want to eat unless they were a rabbit.

"Speaking of health, Jonah," said Dad, "be sure to sign up for a strong athletic program. Tennis, basketball, track. Choose the most active sports."

Just listening to Dad made me very, very tired for some reason. Of course, my parents had been advising me about what to do for a long time, ever since I'd been admitted to Fairlee, but listening to parents' advice is sort of like watching commercials. You know what's coming, you've heard it all before, it's a big bore, but you listen anyway.

Already I had a long list of pluses about being away from my parents, and they were still talking.

"Remember, Jonah, you're going to be living on a certain fixed income, a modest allowance," said Dad. "You'll have to learn to spend your money more judiciously."

Judiciously, how do you like that? He gets some pretty important words into his advice to me.

"It's fortunate that you'll be away from television," said Dad. "It's been an insidious habit, and now you'll be able to break that habit. You'll find that the lack of television will give you extra hours each day, hours you can spend studying and exercising, improving your mind and your body."

"Yes, and I'm glad we've given our television set away," said Mom. "That way, when you come home for vacation, you won't be tempted."

Another double plus for Fairlee. Mom and Dad didn't know it, but the school representative had told me that there was a television set as well as a refrigerator in every room. And there were no rules about watching TV, no time limits. I sighed happily and took out another candy bar. Eating candy bars is one of my most insidious habits.

We were almost at the school now. Dad and Mom would drop me off with my luggage. The last letter from Fairlee—I'd had about fifty of their form letters—had suggested that parents simply leave their kids on the doorstep of the dorm and depart.

"Fairlee has discovered that our new boys are able to adapt more easily and more happily to

*Fairlee life if their first encounter with the
school, the staff, their teachers and their
friends-to-be is made entirely on their own
without the presence of parents or other rela-
tives."*

Of course, the main reason for that, I knew,
was so that the new parents wouldn't find out
that all the rooms were equipped with refrigera-
tors and television sets. There might be other
good surprises, too, things I didn't even know
about yet. Mom's mention of desserts (and how
I should skip them) had given me a very pleasant
feeling. Banana splits, chocolate nut sundaes,
apple pie with ice cream—I sighed happily.

"And it's so nice that your friend from the
apartment building will be your roommate,"
said Mom.

Suddenly all the visions of refrigerator, television, desserts, and freedom went up in a puff of
smoke. Replacing them was a picture of Goober.
Goober, with his repulsive habits, his zillion pimples, and his nonstop interference in my life. I
sighed again, this time in misery.

Goober was worse than my parents because he
spent *all* his time trying to improve me and my

life-style, whereas my parents had other hobbies besides me. Goober Grube, Mr. Holier than Thou, alias Lewis K. Trane. My *roommate*.

I hadn't seen him for about four weeks, so I'd had a chance to get my nervous system calmed down. I still had some pretty harrowing memories, which I'd been trying to forget.

The reason I hadn't seen him lately was that his parents had taken him off somewhere for a vacation right after he and I had been accepted at Fairlee. Maybe he'd changed his mind about coming to Fairlee. Maybe he'd been eaten by a shark. Maybe he'd been arrested for objectionable appearance or behavior or both. Maybe . . . well, I could dream.

I leaned back and shut my eyes, trying to stop thinking about him. I wasn't going to let him spoil anything for me. Actually, it could be worse: Goober might have been twins.

When I opened my eyes again, I saw that we were driving through a big iron gate with big iron letters that spelled FAIRLEE SCHOOL. We were there.

I'd seen so many pictures of Fairlee—the slides that the representative had shown us, and the pictures in all the catalogs and pamphlets they'd been sending—that I felt I'd already been there half my life. We drove up to the dorm, and Dad helped me out with my luggage. We'd been told to bring only two suitcases, so that's all I'd brought. Those and a paper bag with my dwindling supply of candy bars.

All of a sudden my parents were saying goodbye.

"Remember, Jonah, only one helping and no desserts," said Mom, hugging me.

"Don't forget, son," said Dad, shaking my hand, "the most *active* sports."

Next I knew they'd be telling me to be sure to brush my teeth and comb my hair and maybe even to keep breathing, so I waved good-bye, picked up my suitcases, and walked into the dorm.

2 · At First I Thought She Was Going to Bite Me

When I walked into the lobby, I saw a lot of kids standing around looking confused and uneasy. They must all be new kids like me.

I set my suitcases down and held on to my paper bag. There were some adults milling around, smiling very wide smiles, and one of them would soon come over and take charge of me, I was sure.

I didn't see Goober. Good. Maybe he *had* been eaten by a shark. If so, the shark was going to have some very serious problems.

I reached into the paper bag and had just unwrapped a rather soft, mushy chocolate bar when an unusually tall lady with unusually large teeth swooped down on me. At first I thought she was going to bite me, but she didn't.

"Welcome to Fairlee!" she shouted. She grabbed my hand and shook it, and so of course also shook the candy bar, which meant we both got a lot of chocolate on our hands. Her eyes widened and her smile broadened alarmingly.

"You'll want to register, my boy, and then you'll want to go up to your room and unpack." I was to learn that everyone at Fairlee knew what you wanted to do before you did.

"This way," she said, dragging me over to a long table. Some men dressed in blue jackets and big smiles sat on one side of the table, all set to cheer me on my way, get me registered, get me started on the Fairlee path.

"You'll want to sign in, my boy," said the tall lady with the teeth. I wondered what she planned to do with her chocolate-covered hand. Rub me cheerfully on the back, that was it. Clever!

I started at one end of the table and worked my way along. There were forms to sign and catalogs and pamphlets to gather and hands to shake. By the time I was at the end of the table, all the chocolate on my hand had been shared with everyone else.

"Your name," said the last man at the table, raising his bushy black eyebrows.

"Jonah Krock," I said. It was about the fifth time I'd been asked my name, and I wondered if it was some kind of test to see if we remembered our names even when we were far from home and loved ones.

He peered at the list of names in front of him. "Jonah *D*. Krock, right?"

I nodded. I hoped he wouldn't ask what the *D* stood for.

"Now, Jonah, we'll want to know your nickname. We want our boys to feel at home here at Fairlee."

I'd never had a nickname because I never could figure out a really good one, and no one else had ever bothered to make one up for me. I always looked for ideas in the comic books and in the stories about murders in the newspapers. Sometimes you could find good nicknames there, but they just didn't seem to fit me. Elmer "Weasel" Ravell. James "Squealer" Rose. Anthony "Fatso" Ferris. Jack "The Ripper" Flatt. I never found one that suited me.

"I don't have a nickname," I said, and he looked as if I'd announced that I had no nose.

His bushy black eyebrows bristled. "You'll want to have a nickname," he said disapprovingly. Next to my name he wrote, "Nickname to be furnished."

The lady with the large teeth strode over to me. "You're a Fairlee Boy now, my boy, a Fairlee Boy. You'll want to find your room." She turned me around and pointed me to the stairway just like the games of Blind Man's Bluff I'd played when I was two years old. "You'll want to unpack, freshen up, change into your Fairlee colors. Be sure to listen for the bell. It announces the evening meal. The dining hall, as you'll see from the map we have given you, is located in this same building."

I picked up my suitcases and started up the stairs. Second floor. Room 22. I wanted to take a look at that refrigerator. And that television set. I hadn't seen one single program since my parents had given away our television set two weeks ago, and I could hardly wait.

I walked down the corridor, passing about five doors, looking for Room 22. There it was. I set my suitcases down and started to open the door. Something was in the way, so I shoved a little and put my head through the opening.

The wrong room. This was a storage room of some kind. Boxes, books, and clothes were piled all over the place. I backed away to look at the number on the door again.

Then I heard a familiar wheezing and an all-too-familiar voice.

"People should knock before entering," he said. "A man's room is his castle." Goober, of course.

I squeezed through the opening and walked into the room, or rather I climbed in over some of the boxes.

"We were only supposed to bring two suit-cases," I said icily.

Goober was hunched over a desk that was lined with jars and tubes, rubbing something re-pulsive on his face. Four weeks had not im-proved his appearance.

"Anyone can see that all this wouldn't fit into two suitcases," said Goober. "I had a lot of the stuff shipped." He looked around the room, blinking his bulging eyes. "The rest will proba-bly be coming this week."

"And just where am I supposed to put my things?" I asked, raising my voice.

"Anywhere you want to. Just don't move my stuff. I have it all just where I can find it."

The room smelled like a can of sardines. I wondered if he was rubbing fish oil on his face.

I dragged my suitcases in. It wasn't that the room was so small, it was that Goober took up so much of it. Even without all of his junk, his personality filled the place.

Where was the refrigerator? Where was the television set? Two beds, two desks, two chests of drawers, yes, and all of them with Goober's junk covering them, and if I knew Goober, the blankets now on my bed would later be on his.

I stalked around the room, pushing the boxes aside. Aha! Over in a corner, with Goober's clothes draped over it, was a television set. And a (small) refrigerator.

I sighed with relief, pushed Goober's things off to the floor, and opened the refrigerator.

It looked like a medicine cabinet, jammed full of jars and bottles and tubes and—what was *this*, for heaven's sake? It looked like a dead fish. I bent closer. It *was* a dead fish.

I slammed the refrigerator door shut and

turned very slowly around.

"What have you got in our refrigerator?" I asked coldly.

Goober scratched his head, getting the goop that was on his face on his hair, which had been greasy enough to begin with.

"I'm on a new diet," he explained. "A big health program. I have to keep some of my vitamin supplements and supplies in the refrigerator."

"There's a fish in there," I said.

Goober nodded. The billion pimples swam in a sea of oil.

"Smoked chub," he said. "I'm supposed to eat a lot of fish."

I took another look in the refrigerator. There was an open can of sardines. That and the chub helped to account for the alarming odor that was filling the room. And he probably *was* rubbing fish oil on his pimples.

"Tell you what," I said. "I have other ideas for the contents of this refrigerator. Ice-cream bars, chocolate sauce, whipped cream. You know. Banana splits, sundaes, stuff like that."

Goober pursed his lips and closed his bulging eyes. "I'm not interested in junk food anymore," he said piously. "I eat a lot of health foods. And of course fish, as you must know, is brain food. I'm very, very careful of my diet now." He opened his eyes and looked sideways at my stomach. "After all, you are what you eat."

"Well, you can grow up to be a fish if you want," I told him. "I'm planning my future a little differently. Right now, for instance, I'm thinking about having a candy bar. And then I'm going to have another one. And when I've eaten those, I'm planning to buy some more. And some ice cream, and chocolate sauce. And marshmallow sauce and whipped cream. And a lot of things I haven't even thought of yet."

I took one more look in the refrigerator. "A lot of this stuff will have to come out to make room for the stuff I'm going to buy," I told him. I started to push some of his junk to one side. My candy bars were getting pretty soft and mushy. A few minutes in the cold refrigerator would firm them up a little.

"What's this?" I asked suspiciously, pointing to a chunk of something palely disgusting.

"Yeast," explained Goober. "I eat it a lot. It's very, very good for your skin."

"So I see," I said.

"And this stuff," he went on, walking over, standing beside me, and pointing to a huge bottle filled with white stuff. "Drinking this practically guarantees the restoration of the chemical balance of the body."

"That's very interesting," I said. "I can see that you're going to be even more perfect than you already are, if that's possible."

"Actually, no one is really perfect," said Goober, rubbing the ugly ointment on his ugly chin. "But we should all continue to strive to improve ourselves in every way we can."

"That's just what I was saying," I told him. "I want to do the best with this refrigerator that I possibly can. Use it to its capacity."

He stood there, slowly blinking at me. The oily stuff was on his eyelids and eyelashes, and the whole effect was not very pleasant.

I closed the refrigerator door. "I don't like to see it sit idly by. It should be used. That goes for the TV set, too," I said. I looked at the watch Dad had given me. "Yep, it's time for that show I wanted to watch."

"I used to watch television, too," said Goober, walking back to his desk. "But the more I thought about it, the more I realized that the junk I was watching was getting into my brain just as the junk I was eating was getting into my body. I don't watch television anymore. Except for educational programs. I always watch those. You can always learn something from an educational program."

"Is that so?" I asked. "You amaze me with your insights." I turned the switch on the television set. Nothing happened.

"The set isn't hooked up yet," said Goober, annointing his neck. "The reason I know that is that I tried to watch a program myself. An educational program about education. I asked downstairs. They said all the sets would be hooked up tomorrow."

"Oh." I was disappointed. I'd really wanted to watch. No matter *what* was on, I wanted to watch it. Two weeks without television and I was going berserk.

I sighed. I might as well unpack. I opened the closet door. Jammed, of course, with Goober's stuff.

"Look," I said calmly. "We're supposed to share this closet. We're supposed to share this room. I get half, you get half."

"But that isn't fair," whined Goober. "I've got

more things than you have. I need more space."

I didn't bother to answer. I started to push all of the things in the closet to one side. Bundles of clothes, boxes and bags, pillowcases stuffed with heaven knows what.

I don't mind messiness. I like it. But it's one thing to live with my junk and another to live with Goober's. I was only a few minutes into a whole school year, and already I felt crowded.

"Hey," said Goober. "You're messing up all my stuff. I have it all arranged just the way I want it."

"Well, it isn't the way *I* want it," I told him. "You can do anything you like with your half of the closet, and I can do whatever I like with my half."

Goober sighed one of his tragic sighs and walked over to the closet. "I still don't think it's fair for you to get half when I have so much more stuff than you do."

"Life isn't always a bowl of cherries," I told him. "Fairlee Boys have to roll with the punches."

It was true that Goober had more stuff than I had—about fifty times more. I started to hang up some of my things in my half of the closet.

About the Fairlee clothes: The Fairlee logo was an open book with words going around it in a dizzy circle:

KNOWLEDGE IS TRUTH IS KNOWLEDGE
IS BEAUTY IS KNOWLEGDE

The open book, but not the words, was stitched on all of our shirts and blazers. Everything we wore had been ordered specially. Red, white, and navy blue. We were to wear white shirts with blue pants for everyday purposes, red or blue blazers to meals and classes, and all white for Sundays so we'd look pure, like Ivory soap. Our ties were navy blue with the logo stitched in white and red.

The only things that didn't make us look as if we were part of an American flag were our pajamas. We were allowed to wear any color we wanted. Mom had bought mine at a sale, and all of them were an extremely ugly color, the shade, now that I thought of it, of Goober's oddly colored teeth.

I hung everything in the closet and put the extra shoes and sneakers on the floor, so that all I had left in my suitcases were the bilious pajamas, underwear, a lot of socks (red, white, and blue), three ties, and a *TV Guide*. This was the neatest and the best organized I had been in my whole life.

Goober was watching me, blinking and rubbing his chin. "See? You don't need as much room as you think you do," he said.

"Wait till I move in all the ice cream and candy," I told him. "And there's a crate of maraschino cherries on the way."

Of course, Goober had put his things in both chests of drawers. I took out everything from one chest and threw it on his bed. I'd never seen so many tubes, jars, and bottles in my life.

It had taken about half an hour to shove, push, carry, lift, and throw all of Goober's junk to one side of the room. He'd sighed and whined, wheezed and complained the whole time.

I walked over to the refrigerator to retrieve one of the candy bars. It should be nice and firm by now. Nice and firm it was. It also tasted like a chocolate-covered sardine. I muttered something rude under my breath and threw it in the wastebasket.

"I'm glad to see you doing that," said Goober. "That was a wise decision. I think I'm going to be an excellent influence on you. You'll see that as time goes by, your body will react favorably and

you'll lose your taste for junk food. You'll discover that—"

I didn't hear the rest of his sentence. The bell
rang, the bell announcing that there would soon
be a bell announcing dinner.

"Where's a bathroom?" I asked. I'd at least
wash up and put on the Fairlee clothes.

"We have our own bathroom," said Goober,
pointing to a door on his side of the room that I
hadn't noticed before. That was a surprise. The
Fairlee representative, Mr. Bole, had forgotten
to tell me that. I'd thought we'd probably be
sharing a bathroom with a lot of kids, at least the
ones in the room next door.

"Our own TV, our own refrigerator, our own
bathroom," I said. "Pretty neat."

"Yes, those are pleasant amenities," said Goober. He'd learned a lot of new words in three
weeks. "But physical conveniences are just a
minor consideration. The only important thing,
of course, is the quality of instruction. After all,
we are here to learn."

The most important thing for me to learn was
how to live in the same room with Goober without wringing his neck. Or, if I *did* wring it, learn
how to dispose of the body.

I walked into the bathroom. Ointments and creams, caps, lids, and tops, all off and lying around. And a couple of piles of greasy rags on the floor.

Goober was right behind me. "I had to use most of the towels," he said, looking at the rags.

"And what am I supposed to use?" I asked ominously.

"All we have to do is rinse them and wring them out and hang them up to dry," said Goober.

Which is just what I was considering doing with him.

3 · Inch by Ugly Inch

A lot of kids dressed in red, white, and blue were milling around—in the corridor, on the stairs, and in the lobby. Since I'd memorized the map of the dorm, I knew which direction the dining room was, and since I walked as if I knew where I was going, everyone followed me. I felt like the Pied Piper.

Of course, the reason I'd memorized the map was so that I could find the candy bar machines —if necessary, in the dark or blindfolded. They were all lined up on a wall just outside the dining room: food dispensing, calorie-dispensing, happiness-dispensing, coin-operated machines. I'd have to make sure that I had lots of coins all the time.

The tall lady was standing at the entrance to the dining room, showing off her teeth. She handed out cards to us with letters and numbers like A 5, C 7, and so on. That was so we'd all know which table and which seat we were to occupy. Every week we'd get new cards, new numbers, and new tables. The theory was that in this way—changing tables every week—every Fairlee Boy would eventually get to know every other Fairlee Boy, the better to work as a team. I'd read all this stuff and a lot else in the brochures they'd been sending.

Dinner was served cafeteria style, with everyone lining up to get helpings. On a big chalkboard behind the serving counter was a list of what we were having. That was lucky because, since all of it looked pretty much the same, we wouldn't have known what we were eating. We didn't, anyway.

> *"Surprise" Casserole*
> *"Jell-O" Fruit Salad*
> *Banana Bread*
> *Pudding*

There were lots of noodles in the Surprise Casserole, but that was the only ingredient I could identify. The fruit in the Jell-O was sliced bananas. Then there was the banana bread, and the pudding was banana pudding. They must have a good supply of bananas on hand. I wondered whether the unidentifiable objects in the noodle casserole might be bananas, too.

I sat at a table with seven other Fairlee Boys, all of whom looked and talked alike. Maybe they were all related. Or maybe if you went to Fairlee long enough, you all started to look pretty much the same.

The conversation wasn't very stimulating.

"Pass the bread."

"Pass the butter."

"What is this stuff in the casserole?"

"It's mussels," I announced. "Mussels are soft little fish that usually live in shells, although in this case the shells have, of course, been removed."

"Pass the bread."

We played around with our food for a while, had a lot of banana bread, and finally the tooth lady rang a little bell and made some announcements, including the fact that her name was Mrs.

Pomeroy. She was the wife of the headmaster, whose name was *Mr.* Pomeroy.

She told us that tomorrow after breakfast we were to gather in the gymnasium, meet the staff, and select our academic and athletic programs. Classes would start the day after that. We were all proud of being Fairlee Boys, weren't we, and we were going to have a wonderful Fairlee year, and we'd all want to do our very, very best.

As soon as dinner was over, and the announcements, I headed for the machines in the hall. I had enough in my pocket for only seven candy bars. I'd have to get change for that ten-dollar bill that Dad had given me for school supplies.

Since the television set wouldn't be hooked up until the next day, there wasn't much to do when I got back to Goober's and my room. Other Fairlee Boys might be getting acquainted with their new roommates, but I was already too well acquainted with mine, and I didn't relish the prospect of spending much time with him. In the old days it was hard enough to escape Goober, but at least we had lived in different apartments. Now we were in the same *room.*

Goober was muttering to himself: "*I* before *E* except after *C* or when sounding like *A* as in *Neighbor* or *Weigh.*"

I picked up the *TV Guide* to see what I could watch the next day. Lots of new shows coming up. Good.

I tried to concentrate on the new shows, a difficult task since Goober was chanting practically in my ear: "*I* before *E.*"

"Do you absolutely have to talk to yourself?" I asked.

He had rubbed the fish oil off his face and was now applying some goopy white stuff to his pimples.

"In case you are wondering what I'm doing," said Goober (I wasn't), "I'm training my memory. I use all kinds of special techniques to help me remember things. The technical name for this kind of memory aid is m-n-e-m-o-n-i-c. Since the initial *m* is silent . . ." He looked over at me to see if I could understand him or whether he'd have to simplify everything for my sluggish, inferior brain.

He sighed. "The initial *m* is silent," he repeated patiently. "That means the *first m*. The first *m* is silent. So you pronounce it *nee-mawn-ic.*"

"I get it, I get it," I muttered, trying to get back to reading the *TV Guide,* but there was no stopping Goober once he started explaining things.

"I'll give you a very simple example of a mnemonic device," he went on. "Suppose I were trying to remember your first name. Jonah. There are several ways I could proceed." Now he was rubbing the white salve on his neck. Talk about ring around the collar!

"I could think of Jonah and the Whale, for example. Of course, the whale is not really a fish but a mammal, but I could visualize it as being a very big fish, right?"

Which is just the way Goober looked right now, like a very big, very sickly fish.

"So I think of whale," Goober went on. "That reminds me of the word *fish. Fish* remind me of aquariums. Aquariums played a part in our friendship when we first met. So then I can think of your name. Jonah. Jonah and the Whale. See how easy it is?"

"Incredibly simple," I said. "Amazingly uncomplicated."

"Of course, Jonah," he went on, "another way for me to make sure I will remember your name is to use it frequently in conversation. So you see, Jonah, if I say your name as I talk to you, that is a memory reinforcement. An additional mnemonic device, Jonah, to assist me in recalling your name."

"I never understood that before, Goober," I said, "but let me tell you, Goober, I understand it now. You've been very, very helpful to me, Goober, and I want you to know I appreciate your taking the time from your busy schedule to instruct me, Goober."

Goober smiled patronizingly. "It's rewarding to me to see you beginning to accept some of my ideas. At first you were antagonistic. That's understandable. We all are reluctant to accept new concepts, new perceptions, and new perspectives."

He walked over to the closet, reached into one of the pillow cases, and withdrew something that looked like a dead mouse but probably wasn't.

"You may have noticed something different about me," said Goober, carrying the object over to his bed and sitting down again. "It's my hair. I'm wearing it shorter. That's because I don't want any of my psychic energies dissipated. I believe that the longer one's hair, the more energy goes to sustaining it."

I'd never known anyone who had such goofy ideas. "And I'm parting it in the middle now," he went on.

"Very attractive," I lied.

"Thank you. But I did it for experimental, not aesthetic reasons. Parting my hair a new way— in this case, in the middle instead of at the side —may possibly stimulate each individual shaft of hair, which in turn may stimulate the blood vessels that supply it with nourishment. Maybe those blood vessels will in turn stimulate those supplying my brain."

"You'd better be careful," I told him. "You don't want to get too bright. Your brain might electrocute your body."

I turned a page in the *TV Guide*.

I'd been right about the thing in the pillowcase that had looked like a dead mouse: It wasn't. It was a stocking cap.

He started to put it on his head, smoothing it down and fitting it behind his ears. His appearance was not improved.

"At first I used to tape my hair down with

adhesive tape to train it to stay parted in the middle," he said, "but now I use this stocking cap."

A good use for the adhesive tape would have been to tape his mouth shut, but I didn't say anything. I flipped another page in the *TV Guide*.

"A fact you may not have been aware of," said Goober, "is that the human brain has ten billion neurons and one hundred trillion circuit connections. If I discover that parting hair a new way increases the number of those neurons or those circuit connections, then that will be an advance for the human race."

"Knowledge is beauty," I muttered under my breath. I'd be glad when the television set was hooked up so I could listen to it instead of to Goober.

"Experimenting with new ideas of this kind may never have occurred to you," Goober went on. "The fact of your sharing a room with me will, I believe, heighten your own curiosity and lead your mind into new channels of thought."

I'd hate to tell him where my new channel of thought had led me: to the termination of Lewis K. Trane, Jr., alias Goober Grube.

I'd read the *TV Guide* five times. Now I
turned it over and looked at the back cover:

COMING!

BANANA BINGO!

*AN EXCITING NEW CONCEPT IN
TELEVISION VIEWING!*

WIN A THOUSAND DOLLARS

JUST BY WATCHING COMMERCIALS!

A thousand dollars!

I kept reading.

A new program was going to be launched next
week. The program, an amateur variety show
called "Banana Blitz," was to be sponsored by
the American Banana Institute. All you had to do
to win the thousand dollars was to keep track of
the number of times the word *banana* was used
in every commercial. There would be six shows,
one each Wednesday afternoon at two o'clock.
Three commercials to every show.

I got out a pencil and figured it out. Six times
three: eighteen. Eighteen commercials to
watch, and I'd win a thousand dollars. I read it

again. A thousand dollars! And all I had to do was to watch television commercials!

"*I* before *E*, except after *C*," said Goober. "Spelling is a very important ingredient in our Fairlee education."

I kept reading the ad: "Get your BANANA BINGO card at your supermarket TODAY! Only one to a customer. WIN A THOUSAND DOLLARS!"

"These are the exceptions to the spelling rule," said Goober.

It *had* to be my turn to talk, his turn to listen, so I started to tell him about the new program that was going to be sponsored by the American Banana Institute. "All you have to do is to listen to the commercials, mark down on your Banana Bingo card how many times the word *banana* is used, and you get a thousand dollars."

"I was hoping you'd have started to outgrow your bizarre interest in bananas, now that you're at Fairlee," said Goober, "but perhaps that will come in time. Anyway, that Banana Bingo thing sounds kind of fishy to me."

Talk about fishy! He was spearing sardines with a toothpick and swallowing them inch by ugly inch.

"Anyway," said Goober, licking his lips, "you couldn't be sure you'd be able to watch all those programs, all those banana commercials. You might have classes scheduled at those times. Or you might have a conflict with gym or an extracurricular activity or a conference with a teacher. Your responsibilities to your school obligations come first, of course."

Well, that was Goober's very predictable point of view. It wasn't mine.

I lay on the bed and read again about Banana Bingo.

Goober kept munching on the sardines. I could see, hear, smell, and practically taste the whole repulsive procedure.

At the bottom of the page in very small type I read:

> *Banana Bingo cards*
> *may be obtained from*
> *your supermarket with*
> *any fifty-dollar purchase*
> *of bananas.*
> *Only one card*
> *to a customer.*

Fifty dollars! Where would I get fifty dollars? If that was the only way I could get a Banana Bingo card, then I couldn't get a Banana Bingo card.

"With a good education," Goober was saying, "nothing is impossible."

At least Goober had said something sensible: Nothing is impossible. Even getting a Banana Bingo card. I had to have one. I'd find a way.

I'd read the *TV Guide* so many times I'd practically memorized it. The television set wasn't hooked up; there was nothing to do. I walked around the room.

There was a sign on the wall that I hadn't noticed before because Goober had hung his underwear over it.

> *No food on floor*
> *No nails on walls*
> *Don't jump on beds*
> *Don't run in halls*
> *No messy rooms*
> *No undue noise*
> *Remember, you are Fairlee Boys.*

Remember? How could I forget?

I walked around the room a couple more

times, thinking about how I could get a Banana Bingo card. Goober kept muttering to himself. There was nothing to do but put on my ugly pajamas and go to bed.

4 · Maybe He Was Having a Fatal Attack of Pimples

It was pretty hard to get to sleep that first night, what with thinking about getting fifty dollars for a Banana Bingo card and Goober's muttering to himself and thrashing around. But finally I dozed off.

There were going to be a lot of bells at Fairlee: bells in the morning to announce the start of a new Fairlee Day, bells for breakfast, bells before classes and after classes, bells for lunch, bells for assembly, bells for supper, bells for study time, and bells announcing that a bell would soon be ringing. There was a bell for lights-out, too, but

37

ST. MARGARET'S SCHOOL LIBRARY
12664 CENTRAL AVENUE
CHINO, CALIF. 91710

that didn't mean you'd have to turn off television —there were no rules about that. All it meant was that you were supposed to go to sleep. Fairlee Boys were supposed to get a lot of sleep, the better to tackle another Fairlee Day.

Well, you'd think all those bells would be enough bells.

Not for Goober.

Brrrrrrrinnnnnnng! Brrrrrrrinnnnnnng!

I forced my eyes open. Goober was flailing around on his bed trying to find the alarm clock. He knocked it to the floor, where it continued to ring noisily.

"Off," I groaned. "Off with the alarm. I'm still sleeping."

He stumbled out of bed, picked up the clock, shut off the alarm, and said, "If you don't mind my telling you, you've developed some very sloppy speech patterns. You are not, in fact, *still* sleeping. You *were* sleeping. Now that we're here at Fairlee, we should try to speak accurately."

I put my pillow over my head and tried to get back to sleep.

Impossible. Goober was making all sorts of noises, groans, grunts, sighs, moans—maybe he

ST. MARGARET'S SCHOOL LIBRARY
2564 CENTRAL AVENUE
CHINO, CALIF. 91710

was having a fatal attack of pimples or holiness or something.

I peered out from my pillow. He was doing push-ups.

"Ouch, oh, ouch," he was saying now. "Help, that hurts."

I put the pillow back over my head, but it was no use.

"Yikes!" he cried. "Wow!"

"If it isn't too much to ask," I said icily, "if you have to exercise, could you do it silently?"

Another cry of anguish.

Finally it was all over. He sat on the edge of his bed, panting. "It will become easier each time," he assured me. "Beginning a strong exercise program is very strenuous and very painful. The lesson here is that the more it hurts, the better it is for you."

"I want you to know that it hurts me more than it hurts you," I said.

"We must all make every effort to keep our bodies in tiptop condition," Goober went on.

He sounded more like my father than my father did.

He looked at the clock. "The way you begin a day is very important," he said. "I've already had my sitting-up exercises, and the wake-up bell hasn't even rung. That gives me a head start."

It certainly had given his pimples a head start —there were several new interesting ones.

It was too late to try to get back to sleep. I might as well get up and begin a Fairlee Day.

First, breakfast. When I got to the dining room, I looked up at the chalkboard.

> *Cereal with Sliced Bananas*
> *Banana Bread*
> *Banana Fritters*
> *Pineapple Juice*

At least the juice wasn't banana juice. Something told me that would be next.

After breakfast and a couple of announcements, we walked over to the gym because one of the announcements was that we were supposed to. It was a longish walk across campus— I hoped I wouldn't have to see too much of the gymnasium. Fortunately, it was filled with chairs, at least for the moment, so there was no danger of having to do anything more strenuous than sitting down.

We all sat down facing the front, which was a platform, and the same men and women I'd seen last night were sitting on the platform, still smiling the same smiles. Maybe they taped adhesive tape over their faces when they went to bed to keep their smiles in shape.

Goober was sitting right in front of me, so of course I felt right at home.

Everyone on the platform took turns introducing themselves and telling us how great Fairlee was and how very fortunate we were that we had been chosen to be Fairlee Boys. It was a high honor, a proud achievement, a unique privilege, and a lifelong advantage. Everyone was saying the same thing in different words. They had probably all been studying the same book of synonyms or had gone to the same speech class.

"We like to give our Fairlee Boys choices," the man whose eyebrows had been alarmed by the fact that I had no nickname was saying. His name was Mr. Pomeroy. He was the headmaster.

"You are all different, you are all individuals, so of course your tastes vary. Your fields of interest differ. We will want to accommodate you, and of course we anticipate that you will accommodate us."

Everyone was starting to get restless and shifting positions. Mr. Pomeroy understood this to be a wave of applause, and he raised his hands modestly as if to ward off such deserved praise.

"Balance," he went on, after the imaginary applause had subsided, "balance in all things. That's the Fairlee watchword. We nourish your minds, exercise your bodies, we give you well-balanced meals, to physically and intellectually fuel and refuel your systems."

I wondered how he could talk and keep smiling at the same time. Smile really hard and say the word *balance,* for instance. Maybe the guy next to him was a ventriloquist.

The boy next to me had dozed off. I felt my own eyes closing as Mr. Pomeroy droned on. I started thinking again about the fifty dollars I'd need to get a Banana Bingo card.

"Of course, we want to serve the foods that you like the most," he was saying.

My eyes opened.

"Our chef, Mr. Samm, will be available after this meeting, right here in the gymnasium, and I want each and every one of you to come up here and tell him the foods that you most enjoy as well as those to which you might be allergic.

As I've said, here at Fairlee we strive to nourish not only your minds but your bodies."

Mr. Pomeroy must have been the one who'd written all the stuff in the catalog. I'd never known anyone who could keep saying the same thing a hundred different ways. Except Goober, who could out-Pomeroy Mr. Pomeroy any day of the week.

I started to leaf through some of the pamphlets, flyers, brochures, and catalogs in my lap. Maybe Mr. Pomeroy owned a paper factory or a printing press on the side.

YOUR FAIRLEE STAFF

ENGLISH COMPOSITION AND SPELLING	—Mr. Fogarty
AMERICAN HISTORY AND GEOGRAPHY	—Mr. Castor
GREAT LITERATURE	—Mrs. Pomeroy
SCIENCE	—Mr. Sibley
FRENCH	—Mme. Souri
MUSIC	—Mrs. Dixon
ATHLETICS	—Coach Balantine
CHEF	—Mr. Samm
NURSE	—Miss Appleton

Mr. Samm, the chef, was the only one I looked forward to meeting.

In the seat in front of me, Goober was exploring his ears.

The coach talked next, clasping his hands, flexing his biceps, and exercising his muscles as he did so, saying exactly the same sentences I had read in the catalog about building healthy bodies and learning sportsmanship and all that stuff. I expected him to say things like *period, comma, semicolon, new paragraph,* but he didn't.

We were supposed to examine the athletic sheet now, mark our choices of sport, and sign our names.

Goober was making his usual repulsive noises —snuffling, sniffling, swallowing, and wheezing. And as if that wasn't enough, he was whispering to himself, reading out loud: "Badminton, volleyball, tennis, basketball . . ." Much too jumpy for me. I wanted to find something that was not only pretty tranquil but pretty far from Goober. I'd have to get a look at his paper to see which sport he was signing up for so that I wouldn't.

I leaned forward and tapped him on the shoulder, meantime hunching around so that I could get a look at the sheet in his lap.

He turned his head and glared at me. "Sssh!" he hissed. "What do you want? We're not supposed to talk. If we talk, we'll get a demerit. I don't want any demerits on my record. If you get ten demerits by the end of the semester, you lose some of your privileges. I don't want you getting me in trouble like this, talking when we're supposed to be filling in our choices."

He glanced around. "See? Everyone's looking this way. You have to abide by the rules, Jonah, you have to abide by the rules."

I'd had a chance to see the sheet of paper, but I couldn't tell whether he'd marked Weight Lifting or Wrestling, because the X was somewhere in-between. Wrestling! Just the thought of lying on a mat with somebody who was trying to tie me into a pretzel, especially someone like Goober, made me break out in a cold sweat. As for Weight Lifting . . . I sighed and started looking at the top of the list, in the *A*'s, as far away from Goober and the *W*'s as possible. I'd have to find a sport that was pretty quiet. I didn't want to be around any kids who would be throwing balls near me or at me. I didn't want any running, either. No running, jumping, throwing, or being near anyone else who was doing that kind of stuff.

That limited my choices.

Finally I found the perfect sport: Archery. All I'd have to do would be shoot the arrows into the target—or if not actually *into*, at least in the general direction of—and then walk over to retrieve them. And then shoot them all again.

My kind of exercise, my kind of sport. I put a big X next to Archery and heaved a sigh of relief.

5·I Didn't Know and I Didn't Want To Know

The next thing we were supposed to sign up for was Extracurricular Activities. Fairlee Boys were going to be so well rounded they'd bounce.

I looked over the list of possibilities to see whether one of the choices was Watching Television. It wasn't on the list, but Bird Watching was, and I signed up for that. I'm a very good watcher. Probably all I'd have to do was look out of the window once in a while for some bird. I could do that in the mornings while I was getting out of my ugly pajamas and into my Fairlee colors of the day.

The morning seemed pretty long, and it wasn't over yet. As much as I didn't like exercise, I was ready to walk back to the dorm to get a couple of candy bars.

But there were more announcements, and then we had to sing one of the Fairlee songs. There were dozens of them. All the words to all the songs were in one of the pamphlets they'd passed around: *Fairlee Songs for All Occasions*. The tune of this one was much like "The Farmer in the Dell."

> *A Fairlee Boy is strong*
> *A Fairlee Boy is true*
> *A Fairlee Boy's a special boy*
> *A Fairlee Boy is YOU!*

Then there was a lot of milling around, and the teachers and advisers were all shaking hands with each other and with as many Fairlee Boys as possible. It was sort of like an athletic event that Fairlee had just won.

Finally it was time to talk to the chef about my favorite foods. This was going to be the best part of the whole day, so far.

There were a lot of guys ahead of me in line, so while I waited I entertained myself by thinking about that Banana Bingo game and how I could possibly get fifty dollars to buy the bananas that would entitle me to a Banana Bingo card.

Finally it was my turn to talk to the chef, Mr. Samm.

He was a forlorn-looking guy, with pale hair hanging over pale, sad eyes.

"How do you do, Mr. Samm," I said graciously. Being polite is one of the hallmarks of a Fairlee Boy. I'd read that sentiment at least sixty times.

"Call me Sammie," he said. "Everybody else does.

"O.K., Sammie," I said politely.

He had a chart in front of him, and he'd been marking down everyone's favorite foods as well as their allergies. He glanced at the chart.

"So far I've had nine requests for pizza, six for hamburgers, and twelve for weenies. And one," he added dolefully, "for fish."

I could guess where *that* had come from.

"Sardines and tripe," said Sammie. "Do you know what tripe is?"

"Oh yes," I lied. I didn't know, and I didn't want to know.

Most of the other boys had left the gymnasium and were probably wandering back toward the dorm. A picnic was scheduled for our noon meal today. The staff members were talking and assembling the papers we'd turned in with our choices of sports and extracurricular activities.

I noticed that Mr. Pomeroy was walking in my direction.

"I'm supposed to serve a wide variety of foods," said Sammie. "And I'm supposed to provide alternative menus on those occasions when a food is served to which one of our boys might be allergic." His pencil was poised anxiously over his chart.

If I was allergic to anything, it was to Goober and his sardines.

Mr. Pomeroy came up, waving his eyebrows. "Have you decided on a nickname yet?" he asked.

It was at that moment that Sammie posed his question: "What are you allergic to?"

"Fish," I said, thinking of Goober.

Sammie wrote it down in the space next to my name while Mr. Pomeroy nodded approvingly. "Splendid. All of our Fairlee Boys have nicknames. You wouldn't want to be an exception. Having a nickname is part of the flavor of being a Fairlee Boy."

So my nickname was going to be Fish. One more headache to bear because of Goober.

"And what is your favorite food?" asked Sammie, ready to finish filling in the chart. Thinking about the nickname, I almost said "Fish" but caught myself in time.

"Next to candy bars and sundaes," I told him, "I like bananas."

He brightened. "Bananas? Really? *Really?* That's very reassuring. Because I have many, *many* bananas on hand. The salesman was very, *very* persuasive. I'm afraid I overordered. And there's not much to do with bananas except eat them. I mean, you can't freeze them or anything. They're just . . . there. I have to use them up right away."

I couldn't help feeling kind of sorry for this guy.

Sammie shook his head sadly. "This is my first week working at Fairlee. The only reason they *hired* me in the *first* place was that I was a Fairlee Boy. And I'm the only Fairlee Boy who decided to be a chef." He sighed. I hope he wasn't going to burst into tears or anything.

"Now here I am," he went on, "stuck with all these bananas. I shouldn't have ordered so many," he said. "But the salesman told me that if I ordered a *lot* of bananas, I could enter some special sweepstakes or something. If I won, I'd get a thousand dollars. The mention of a monetary reward was very tempting."

I started listening—hard.

"He told me that all I have to do in order to win the money would be to listen to some commercials about bananas and mark down how many times the word *banana* is used each time. If the card is completed accurately, I would win a thousand dollars."

He blinked. "Well, now I have the card and I also have this big supply of bananas."

My ears were pricking up so much during this conversation that they were tingling. This guy had a Banana Bingo card!

He kept talking. "Of course, after I'd agreed to buy the bananas, I realized that I wouldn't have time to watch all those banana commercials. There's no television set in the kitchen, and that's where I usually am. So it was all for nothing. I have so many bananas in the kitchen that I'm going bananas. I can't think of very many ways to use them."

"Oh, I can," I said quickly. "I'll be glad to help

you come up with a lot of ideas for using them up."

"Really?" he asked, brightening. *"Really?"*

"No problem," I told him. "In fact, I can work on a list right away. Today."

"I really, *really* appreciate that," said Sammie. He smiled, and it was the most sincere smile I'd seen since I arrived at Fairlee.

"Thank you. That would be wonderful. If there's anything I can do for you—"

"As a matter of fact, there is," I said quickly. "Not only am I very, very interested in bananas, I am also interested in Banana Bingo." I took a deep breath. "You have a Banana Bingo card, but you won't be able to watch the commercials. I can watch all the commercials, but I don't have a Banana Bingo card." I paused, waiting for him to get the message.

He got it.

"Why don't I give you my card and then we could share the money we'd win?" he said. Share, I thought. It would be nice to have the whole thing. But it was share or nothing.

It was my turn to smile. Talk about sincere!

Half of a thousand dollars!

"That way we'll each win five hundred dollars," I said. My math seemed to be improving.

If Fairlee ever had a contest for sincere smiles, Sammie and I would win, hands down.

"It so happens," I said modestly, "that I am very good at watching television. I'm sort of an expert. I'll watch every single banana commercial, and I won't miss a single mention of the word *banana*. You can count on me."

"You've made my day, Jonah," said Sammie. "Really made it." He reached into his pocket. "I'll give you the card right now." He handed it to me and I examined it carefully. It had all the dates of all the shows, and there were spaces to mark down the number of times the word *banana* was used in each commercial. It would be a snap. No problem.

I'd mark all the dates and times on a calendar and make sure that nothing would interfere. Banana Bingo would come first. No matter what.

I was the last one left in the gymnasium.

"You'll get that list of ways I could serve bananas, won't you?" Sammie asked anxiously.

"By breakfast tomorrow," I promised. "Of course, as you probably know, an excellent way to use up lots of bananas is in banana splits."

He nodded. "The thing is," he said worriedly,

American Banana Institute

WATCH! BANANA BLITZ!

PLAY! BANANA BINGO!

WIN! A THOUSAND DOLLARS!

Check the number of times the word banana is used (spoken or sung).

		Commercial I	Commercial II	Commercial III	Total
Sept. 8	B				
Sept. 15	A				
Sept. 22	N				
Sept. 29	A				
Oct. 6	N				
Oct. 13	A				
BINGO!					

"I've used up so much of the food budget on bananas that I don't have enough money left to buy much of anything else. Like ice cream, for instance. Or cherries. Or any of those nuts or sauces."

"Oh," I said. After all, a banana split isn't a banana split without all the other stuff.

On the way back across the campus I thought about the Banana Bingo card. Now I had it, and all I had to do to make five hundred dollars was to watch all of those shows. Or at least all of those commercials. Simple. I was beginning to like Fairlee. A lot.

6 · My Brain Is Working All the Time

Nothing except the picnic was scheduled for the rest of the day because we were supposed to have a chance to get acquainted with the Fairlee campus and with all the Fairlee catalogs and pamphlets and Fairlee customs and Fairlee Boys. Classes would begin tomorrow.

The picnic consisted of some more songs, some more smiles, and peanut butter and banana sandwiches. When it was finally over, I headed for the dorm. I could hardly wait to get back up to the room to see whether they'd activated our television set. And of course, I was

ready for another candy bar. I'd put several in
our refrigerator, this time wrapped in aluminum
foil to keep out the fishy taste from Goober's
sardines. My ten dollars was dwindling fast.

When I opened the door, Goober was sitting
on the edge of his bed in bare feet, eating sardines again. They were spilling over his chin,
and the room smelled like a fish factory. I
grabbed a candy bar from the refrigerator,
walked over to the television set, and turned it
on. It worked. Good. There were only two channels and nothing very exciting was on, but it had
been so long since I'd watched at all that anything looked good. And of course, the more you
watch television, the better everything seems, so
that after a while it all looks good, even the commercials and the station announcements.

And I was a good enough television watcher,
even with that long interval away from it, to be
able to do something else while I was watching
and not miss a thing.

I took out the Banana Bingo card that Sammie
had given me and examined it again, keeping
part of my brain on the stupid TV show that was
on and was already half over. Then I pulled the
Fairlee calendar out of the piles of paper pro-

ducts they'd given us ("Make Every Fairlee Day Count") and looked at that.

September and October were the important months, the Banana Bingo months.

The Fairlee calendar was filled with all sorts of Fairlee activities, but of course nothing that was nearly as urgent as watching the banana commercials. I filled in the calendar with the dates and times of every show. I wouldn't miss a single one. It would mean I'd have to miss Mrs. Pomeroy's class each Wednesday, but I'd work *that* out.

Goober finished the last of the sardines in the can. I wondered whether he'd use the remaining oil for his pimples.

Nope, he poured what was left into his ugly mouth.

I taped the calendar and the Banana Bingo card over my desk. There, that was done, and I hadn't missed a single thing on the stupid show that was on television. Watching television is like riding a bike; once you've learned how, you never lose the knack.

A game show was on next, and I watched it while I started to make the list for Sammie of the ways he could use up all those bananas.

I decided to have separate columns: Bananas as a Main Course would be one. And of course there would be a column for Banana Desserts. I wrote that down.

Then I tried to think of ways that Sammie could fix bananas.

"What are you doing?" asked Mr. Repulsive, walking over to my desk and looking over my shoulder.

"Watching this show on television," I told him.

"It's just a game show," he said, trying to get a look at my paper. I flipped the paper over and concentrated on the show. He sighed and went back to sit on his bed.

"You should watch an educational program," he said. "Improve yourself."

"I happen to like situation comedies, crime shows, reruns of old series, cartoons, and game shows," I said. "I do not happen to like educational programs. Educational programs happen to have nothing happening. No plot, no story."

Goober opened his mouth to interrupt. I was afraid I might see a last sardine swimming around in there, so I hurried on. "I know what you're going to say," I said. "You're going to say that there's no plot in a game show, either. Well, that's the exception that proves the rule. I'm sure you're familiar with *that* rule, which is that there is always an exception to every rule."

He blinked. His mouth was still open.

"Game shows are exciting," I went on. "You can get into the spirit, you can participate. With educational programs you can't do anything but fall asleep."

"That's not true," said Goober. "You learn a lot from educational programs. You don't learn anything from game shows or all that other junk you watch."

"You'd be surprised," I said. "My brain is working all the *time* trying to assimilate all the information that game shows give me. I could get an A on any trivia quiz."

Goober swallowed, and his Adam's apple bobbed around. I'd been right: He must have had a sardine floating around in there somewhere.

"We're here at Fairlee to learn," said Goober in his most holy way. "To learn, to expand our minds, and to perfect our skills. To enlarge our horizons."

"Maybe they could hire you to write the copy for the next catalog," I suggested.

"That has already occurred to me," said Goober. "I've been considering many possibilities. Our brains should always be receptive to new ideas. We must keep an open mind."

With Goober, an open mind also meant an open mouth.

"We must struggle to make the most of our opportunities," he went on piously. "Speaking for myself, I always strive to do the best I can, although I admit I have not attained perfection."

"Modesty is one of your most noble traits," I told him.

"Thank you, Jonah," said Goober. "It strikes me that you yourself are improving. You've learned to make gracious remarks about others. You used to resist such impulses."

I didn't tell him that the impulse I was now resisting was to push his face into that open mouth.

Goober started to put on his socks, one blue and one red.

"Your socks don't match," I told him.

"It doesn't matter," said Goober. "It doesn't say anywhere in the rules that your socks have to match."

"And it doesn't say anywhere that you can't

drown your roommate in the bathtub, either," I said.

Goober shook his head sadly.

"I feel that your aggressive impulses are due to watching so much violence on television," he said.

"I never thought of that," I said. "You really have reached a very original conclusion. I'm sure educators and psychiatrists and parents all over the country would like to hear your opinion."

I looked at my list. I had a column for bananas as a main course and a column for banana desserts.

MAIN COURSE	DESERT
Banana Stew	Banana Turnovers
Banana Shish Kebob	Banana Cream Pie
Barbecued Bananas	Banana Cookies
Baked Bananas	Banana Sherbet
Braised Bananas	Candied Bananas
	Banana Mousse

Goober picked up the list. He read it over, moving his lips. "You didn't spell *dessert* right," he said, frowning. "It has two *s*'s."

"I know," I lied. "This is just my scratch copy. I left the extra *s* out to save time."

He didn't believe me.

"Here's a good way to remember which is *desert* and which is *dessert,*" he said. "*Desert* has only one *s* because you're hot and thirsty and you're hurrying to get through it, see? And *dessert* has two *s*'s because it tastes so good you want to linger over it. It's that simple. Remember, you can work out a mnemonic device for everything."

He looked back at my list. His frown deepened. Every time he frowned, the pimples on his forehead rearranged themselves. There was no improvement in his appearance, however.

"Plain," he said. "You forgot plain."

I didn't know what he was talking about, but that was nothing new.

"Plain," he repeated. "Just a regular banana. Peeling the skin down partway, biting into the banana the way you'd bite into an ice-cream bar, then peeling the skin down a little more, taking another bite, and so on. And then, of course," he added smugly, "remembering to dispose of the skin properly."

"Yes, of course I'd thought of that," I lied. "But

then I had the additional thought that serving plain bananas would mean ending up with a lot of banana peels on the tables. And that provided me with the further thought that banana peels on the tables might soon become banana peels on the floor. And a fact about banana peels that may have escaped your notice is that they are slippery when stepped on."

Goober was about to interrupt, as was his custom, so I hurried on.

"Visualizing that simple progression of events, then, led me to the conclusion that serving plain bananas might lead to a series of unfortunate accidents, and I felt it was my duty to do everything in my power to prevent that possibility. Therefore, I have omitted plain bananas from my list of banana possibilities. As you might gather, and rightfully so, I have given this matter some thought."

Every time Goober doesn't like the way the conversation is going, he tries to channel it differently. Now he tried to get back to spelling because he thought he knew more about it than I did.

"One of the ways I can help you is to show you how to improve your spelling," said Goober.

"For instance, the difference between *there, they're,* and *their.*" Of course, the way he said it, they all sounded the same.

"The way I remember," Goober went on, "is to remind myself—"

"Oops!" I interrupted. "There's a program coming on right now. A program I can't possibly miss."

Goober pursed his lips disapprovingly. "I was going to tell you a rule that would help you all your life," he said. "Whereas a television program—unless, of course, it's an educational instructional program—lasts just as long as it lasts."

"That's a very philosophical remark," I said, "and I'll be sure to remember it. *A program lasts just as long as it lasts.* It's amazing that you can continue to come up with such perceptive observations."

He smirked a Gooberlike smirk. Other people smirk, but no one can smirk like Goober.

There wasn't going to be much on TV tonight, according to my *TV Guide,* but I wanted to watch anyway. After all, those American Banana Institute commercials were going to be starting on Wednesday, and I had to be ready.

7 · The Way You Phrase Things Is Very, Very Important

All of the classes at Fairlee were held in a building about a hundred yards from the dorm. It seemed like a hundred miles. They should have had those moving sidewalks like the ones I'd seen at a couple of airports, where all you have to do is to step on and then step off. And they should have put in escalators or elevators so we wouldn't have to climb all those stairs. It was a sort of backward school in that respect.

As soon as classes were over on Tuesday, I hurried back to the dorm and dinner. According to my calculations (I was getting lots of chances to use my math skills these days), Sammie had used up three hundred bananas so far.

Walking down the corridor to Room 22, I noticed that they'd put name plates on all the doors:

> GILBERT L. TRENT
> "GIB"
>
> ALFRED E. LANGFIELD
> "SNUFFY"
>
> LEWIS K. TRANE
> "GOOBER"
>
> JONAH D. KROCK
> "FISH"

I knew that nickname would follow me around the rest of my life. It would be like having Goober always at my heels. I sighed.

I was out of money and nearly out of candy bars. And I really needed one right now. Goober was sitting on his bed cutting his toenails. I flicked on the television set on my way across the room. When I opened the refrigerator I saw that I was down to three candy bars, and probably all of them tasted fishy by now, in spite of the aluminum foil. I bit into one. I was right.

I lay down on my bed and ate it while I watched a commercial about dentures. I tried to figure out a way to get some more money, just to tide me over while I was waiting for the five hundred dollars, which I wouldn't be getting until all the banana programs were over, which would be a month from now.

I'd have to get the money from Dad. There wasn't any other way. If I called him up, he'd be sure to ask me about my athletic involvement, and since the only exercise I'd had since I'd arrived at Fairlee was running out of candy bars, I decided to write a letter. I turned down the volume on the television set, got out a pad and pencil, and started:

Dear Dad,
I'm afraid I'm running out of cash,
haha

was as far as I got when Goober said, "Very commendable, Jonah. Somehow I was confident that the time would come when you would grow to recognize the lasting value of establishing strong study habits. This marks a very important turning point in your academic career, Jonah."

I rolled my eyes and tried to concentrate on my letter and of course on the television program.

"The significance of turning away from the television set and toward your desk has not escaped me. It is indeed a symbolic gesture."

I glanced over at Goober. He seemed to be putting some fish oil on his toes, but I couldn't be sure. He misinterpreted the glance.

"I know you're embarrassed, Jonah, about thanking me for the part I have played in this change in your priorities. That's perfectly understandable. It's difficult to admit to anyone, Jonah, sometimes even to yourself, that an idea you had opposed vigorously has a great deal of merit after all. And it's often next to impossible to bring yourself to thank an erstwhile opponent. I understand. The fact that I have served as a role model and was therefore instrumental in focusing your attention on the importance of studying and learning is gratifying to me. I only hope . . ." Goober rattled on, and I started my letter to Dad all over again:

Dear Dad,
   You will be gratified to know, Dad, that thanks to you, who have been an important

role model, I have grown to recognize the lasting value of establishing strong study habits. You have been instrumental in my decision to focus my attention on the importance of studying and learning. I have changed my priorities. Turning away from the television set and toward my desk is more than a symbolic gesture. It is an indication of the direction my life is now taking. This is a very important turning point in my academic career, Dad, and I want you to know that, hard as it is to admit to anyone, even to myself, I now realize that an idea I had opposed vigorously has a great deal of merit after all.

P.S. Just as an afterthought: in my new academic endeavors, I will need some basic supplies. Will you please send along a few dollars to enable me to purchase them.

I glanced again over at Goober, who was now putting the stocking cap over his ugly head.

I added to my postscript: "It's unfortunate that money has to rear its ugly head, but such, alas, is the case." There. I wanted to write a letter to Mom, too, but my next program was about to come on, and I didn't want to miss it. I wrote,

"Tell Mom that I am remembering her very sound advice about no second helpings and no desserts."

That wasn't a lie, actually, because I did remember her advice. The way you phrase things is very, very important.

While I was watching the next program, I put on my ugly pajamas and sat on the edge of the bed.

"Instead of watching television," said Goober, "you should be learning something. For instance, you've heard me memorizing a rule for spelling: *I* before *E* except after *C* or when sounding like *A* as in *Neighbor* or *Weigh.*"

"Oh, yes, I've heard you," I told him.

"Well, here are the exceptions to this rule," he said, eyeing a paper that he was holding with a greasy hand. "Either, neither, leisure, height, foreign, seize, and weird."

There was nothing like listening to Goober to make a person really tired.

"Memorizing a list of random words seems at first glance a difficult task," Goober went on. "But that difficult task is simplified by applying one of my memory aids. For example, they may be easily remembered with this easily remembered sentence: *Foreigners* may *seize* upon their *leisure* moments *either* to reach new *heights* or to do something *weird,* or *neither.*"

He looked up proudly. "Now all I have to do is commit this simple sentence to memory, and I will forever after know how to spell these difficult words."

"Incredible," I said. "Fantastic."

"I'm happy to share all of my shortcuts to knowledge with you," said Goober grandly. "After all, we're roommates, and roommates should share."

"I'm willing to share some of my shortcuts with you, too," I told him. "For example, you may find the word *banana* hard to spell. How many *n*'s? How many *a*'s? With this memory aid, which I am patenting, you will never again have difficulty with this particular word."

I thought for a moment, and then I said:

> *Three a*'s, two *n*'s, one *b*
> That spells *banana,* as you can see.

"I think you're beginning to get the general idea," said Goober graciously. "With practice, you'll improve, of course."

"You've set such a shining example," I said. "I

can only strive to emulate you."

Emulate was a word *I'd* learned in the past four weeks. Goober wasn't the only big brain to arrive at Fairlee.

8·I Wasn't Really Lying

On Wednesday I walked into Mrs. Pomeroy's class a few minutes early. That meant I'd had to simulate a coughing spell toward the end of Mr. Castor's class (American History and Geography) so I could get out of that before the bell rang. After my prolonged bout of coughing, Mr. Castor had smiled sympathetically and said, "You may be excused from class, Jonah. There's a water bubbler down the hall."

I'd nodded through my cough and left the room, with many envious eyes on my back, I knew. I'd have to try something else the next time, because something told me that lots of Fairlee Boys would be having lots of coughing attacks as time went by.

When I walked into Mrs. Pomeroy's room, she was sitting at her desk getting all psyched up for the class ahead by reading something *really* boring: *Ivanhoe*.

She looked up as I walked into the room, and her teeth flashed into view.

"Good afternoon, Mrs. Pomeroy," I said politely, flashing my own teeth, or rather my braces. I took a deep breath. "I'm afraid I have a problem today, Mrs. Pomeroy. And the problem is that I must telephone home at promptly two o'clock. And two o'clock, of course, is the time of your very interesting and informative class in Great Literature, which I will be very, very disappointed to have to miss."

She started to say something, but I hurried (politely) on. "This is my problem, Mrs. Pomeroy, and I know you will understand. My elderly aunt, who regards me as her favorite nephew, is very, very ill and must leave this afternoon for Europe for her health. The doctor has requested that I telephone her before she does, and I know you understand the psychological and physical benefits that she will derive from hearing my voice and that you of course would not want me to go against the express wishes of her physician."

"Of course," murmured Mrs. Pomeroy, her teeth for the moment subdued. "Of course *not*," she added. "You may be excused, Jonah."

I wasn't really lying. Mom's sister Janice, who's thirty-five if she's a day, was really going to Europe and I am her only nephew, and therefore her favorite one. Her husband is a doctor and he *always* likes me to call them up, and this time would be no exception, I was sure. And of course, I hadn't really *said* I was going to call her, because I wasn't. As for her being very ill—well, the last time I'd talked to her she had a cold. I'm very, very careful about telling the truth whenever possible. It's not what you say, it's how you say it.

It was a brisk walk back to the dorm, and I was out of breath by the time I got up to the room. I turned on the television set, grabbed my chart, and settled down to watch the first show. A disembodied voice announced: "The American Banana Institute is proud to bring you 'Banana Blitz'!" (Two bananas so far, and I marked that down.) Then there were a lot of razzle-dazzle lights and a shot of the smiling faces of the amateur singers and dancers, comedians and acrobats, who were to appear on this program.

Some guy started to talk about bananas and
the American Banana Institute ("Better Bananas
Today for a Better World Tomorrow"), and he
mentioned the word *banana* eight times. The
middle commercial was a singing commercial,
four guys singing a barbershop quartet:

> *Yes, we do like bananas,*
> *We do like bananas, we do.*
> *Yes, we all like bananas,*
> *Bananas are so good for you!*

That wasn't hard (four bananas), but the cho-
rus of puppets in the shape of bananas that followed it was pretty tricky:

> *Banana, nana, nana, bananabee*
> *Banana, nana, nana, banana-nanna-bee*
> *Anna, banana, bananabee!*

O.K. Six in that one.

The show itself, with amateur amateurs doing
things in a very amateurish way, was unusually
terrible. No wonder they had to bribe everyone
to watch the commercials. Otherwise no one
would have watched the show.

The rest of the program was just as sappy as
the commercials. After everything was over, a

deep voice said, "This week's program of 'Banana Blitz' is brought to you by the American Banana Institute."

That counted as part of the last commercial, so I changed the score. I marked the Banana Bingo card and taped it back on the wall over my desk.

"Want to know an easy way to remember all the Great Lakes?" asked Goober that night.

"Not especially," I said.

"Think of the word *HOMES*. That's all you have to do. H-O-M-E-S. Huron, Ontario, Michigan, Erie, Superior. Easy, isn't it?"

"You bet," I said. Actually, I couldn't get that dumb banana jingle out of my head. Yes, I do like bananas.

"Yes, I do like the Great Lakes," I muttered under my breath.

"There's another way I've figured out to remember them," said Goober, wiping his fishy hands on his shirt. "It's sort of a poem. Listen:

Whichever Great Lake you're on
Michigan, Erie, or Huron
Superior or Ontario,
You'll love it when you are there-ee-oh.

"You like it?" he asked anxiously.

"It's beautiful," I told him. "It really gets you, you know that?"

"I made it up this morning while I was doing my sitting-up exercises," said Goober. "That way I'm not wasting a minute. My brain is working right along with my body."

I changed channels. If only Goober were a television program instead of a roommate, so I could turn him on and off.

Goober kept talking. "Of course, it would be simpler for me if I watched television a lot, the way you do, but my academic achievements must take priority."

I wondered what the inside of Goober's brain looked like, with all those words ricocheting around in it and coming out of his mouth in various arrangements.

A commercial about indigestion was over, so I turned the volume up. Goober sighed deeply. "I'm beginning to think you came to Fairlee just to watch television," he said.

"That's a very perceptive remark," I told him. "As it happens, that was only one reason for my desire to attend this school. The other reason, of course, was so that I could room with you and observe your habits and benefit by daily exposure to your ideas."

"Thank you," said Goober with a smirk. "Although I sense that your remark is partly in jest, it does demonstrate an undercurrent of real appreciation. In exaggeration there is often to be found a core of truth."

I tried to concentrate on the television program. It was pretty boring, but not as boring as those dumb amateurs on the "Banana Blitz" program.

Goober was rummaging through all of his boxes and bags and pillowcases, finding new salves and ointments with which to annoint himself.

"I am positive that you can benefit from our close association," he said. "I want to show you how a memory device can help you with your homework and your efforts to excel."

I dragged my eyes away from the television just in time to see him apply the white ointment to his bulging forehead. I looked back at the program.

"The Boston Tea Party, for instance, which we're studying in history class now. We all know, of course, what that was about, but do we recall the exact year?" He paused a split second and then went on. "It was in seventeen seventy-three. Now we have many, many dates to remember. Dates of the Revolutionary War, dates of the Declaration of Independence, and so on. How will we remember the date of the Boston Tea Party?" He paused dramatically. "How about this?" he went on. "It's seventeen seventy-three, we won't pay the tax on the tea." He waited for my comment, which was not forthcoming. "See?" he asked. "It rhymes. *Tea* and *three* rhyme."

"Beautiful," I said. "Simply beautiful."

"You never know when a fact like that will help you," said Goober. "You never know when you're going to be called upon to furnish a date of that kind."

As I dozed off that night, I could still hear Goober:

It's seventeen seventy-three
We won't pay the tax on the tea
Let's throw all the tea in the sea
For we won't pay the tax on the tea
We won't pay the tax, we won't pay the tax
In seventeen seventy-three.

I put my pillow over my head and finally fell asleep.

But not for long.

Goober turned on his light and I jumped awake.

For a minute I thought I was dreaming because he looked like something from under a rock or from out in space with his bulgy eyes and bulgy pimples sticking out of the white-ointment face and his teeth glowing and that stocking cap.

"Hope I didn't disturb you," he said. "I had to remind myself of one of my memory aids." He picked a paper off the floor and studied it, moving his lips. I turned over so I couldn't see him, but of course I could still hear him.

"It's very important to the learning process to think of something you want to memorize as you're falling asleep," he said. "For a moment I'd forgotten my sentence. Now, if I say it over three times, it will be mine forever."

I groaned. "Haven't you read that sign about undue noise?" I asked.

". . . or when sounding like *A* as in *Neighbor* or *Weigh* . . ."

Neigh, I thought, as I tried to go to sleep. Goober did look a little like an old horse. An ugly one.

"... *Foreigners* may *seize* upon their *leisure* moments ..."

I finally went back to sleep. I got awake in the middle of the night, thinking an ugly horse had indeed found its way into our room, but it was only Goober snoring. Snoring!

9 · A Real Fairlee Boy Wasn't Supposed To Have a Real Sense of Humor

Mr. Castor had been talking a lot to us about American History and Our Proud Heritage and a lot of other stuff that I didn't want to hear about. We had a textbook that said the same things a slightly different way. It was probably the most boring book ever written. Facts and dates, names of places you'd never want to know about, and activities of people who'd died about a billion years ago.

Today Mr. Castor stood in front of the room

smiling without showing his teeth. He never showed his teeth when he talked, either.

"I have a surprise for you today, class," he said. "It's a spring quiz."

A quiz. I sighed. Now I wished I'd studied last night instead of watching television.

He paused. "Why do I call it a spring quiz, you ask. After all, it's fall." He smiled mysteriously for a minute and then he said, "I call it a spring quiz because I am *springing* it on you. Hence the expression *spring quiz.*"

I glanced over at Goober, who was smiling smugly. He was probably the only one in the whole room who had studied.

Mr. Castor went on. "At Fairlee we are not, as you will discover, devotees of the true-and-false, fill-in-the-blank, multiple-choice school of thought. That sort of quiz does not encourage original expression. An essay quiz, on the other hand, calls upon our own individual powers of verbalizing our ideas."

He turned to the chalkboard.

"Get out your pens and papers while I write your essay subject on the board."

I looked around the room. Everyone was looking blank.

Everyone but Goober.

The guy sitting at the next desk, a thin kid with droopy hair, leaned over and whispered, "Some kids who've been to Fairlee before told me that Mr. Castor never really reads all the papers. He just notices how *much* you've written, not *what* you've written. They said as long as you stay on the general subject, so if he glances over it, he'll see some words he wants to see, you're O.K."

I hoped he was right.

Mr. Castor wrote: "Tell what you know about the Boston Tea Party."

For a second I was tempted to write *Nothing*, but a real Fairlee Boy wasn't supposed to have a real sense of humor. I looked over at Goober, who was already writing busily.

I wracked my brain to remember something, anything. *The Boston Tea Party,* I wrote.

I tried to get a look at the paper of the guy sitting next to me. He must know what he was writing about. He had very neat handwriting, so it was easy for me to read what he wrote:

Tea is a beverage which can be served either hot or iced, hence the expression "iced tea."

I sighed and wished for the first time that Goober sat closer to me. I looked again at the paper of the kid at the next desk:

A common custom in these times is to put the tea leaves into "bags," hence the expression "tea bags." The Boston Tea Party took place in Boston, hence the expression "Boston Tea Party."

I stopped reading his paper and started to write my own. I tried to remember just what it was that Goober had been mumbling last night. Suddenly I remembered: "It's seventeen seventy-three, we won't pay the tax on the tea."

I breathed a sigh of relief and started to write:

Needless to say, the Boston Tea Party was held in Boston. The date was 1773, a date we remember because—

I paused and considered.

—a date we remember because it is a date we do not want to forget: the date of the Boston Tea Party, a historical and memorable occasion.

What else had Goober been mumbling about? I couldn't remember. Just "It's seventeen seventy-three, we won't pay the tax on the tea."

I wrote on:

We wouldn't pay the tax on the tea. Even in seventeen seventy-three, people did not like taxes. In fact, there is in recorded history nothing to indicate that at any time people really enjoyed paying taxes. Seventeen seventy-three was no exception.

I wracked my brain to think of something else I could write. I glanced again over at Goober, who was writing and moving his lips. What else had he been saying last night? Suddenly I remembered: "Let's throw all the tea in the sea, for we won't pay the tax on the tea."

I started writing again:

We did not want to pay the tax on the tea. To demonstrate our dislike of the aforementioned tax, we threw all the tea into the sea. Now, remembering that this was seventeen seventy-three, the "we" I refer to is a group of people who, alas, are no longer alive. However, be-

cause of their strong feelings against taxes on tea, we remember their actions to this day, even though this event occurred in seventeen seventy-three. Now, whenever we hear the words "Boston Tea Party," we think of tea, of taxes, and of seventeen seventy-three. The date lives in our memories and in history.

I looked up. Everyone was looking at me, probably because I was still writing and they had run out of things to say.

Mr. Castor was beaming at me and nodding. Goober was regarding me with new respect in his bulgy eyes.

I signed my paper.

"Now, class, as you leave the room, leave your papers on my desk. It gives me much pleasure to see that some of you"—he looked in my direction—"have studied and have been able to express what you have learned in written words of your own choosing. It is to be hoped that we will *all* learn during these forthcoming weeks to express ourselves on paper with confidence."

He rattled on for a few minutes, seeing how many times he could say the same thing in different words. Probably when he was my age, he'd been good at essay questions, too. Maybe I'd be a teacher when I was *his* age.

Goober caught up to me as we walked out of class. "You must have really been paying attention in class, after all," he said. "Because you had a lot of information to write down about the Boston Tea Party, and I know you haven't opened that history textbook once."

"Oh, it wasn't anything," I said modestly. "Once I fix something in my mind, it's mine forever."

"You certainly had me fooled," he said. "I thought you wouldn't be able to remember a thing about the Boston Tea Party. You must have a very, very good system."

"Oh, I do," I said grandly. "Rooming with me will be an educational experience for you."

Our grades were in our mailboxes the next day. I opened the envelope. I got an A, and Mr. Castor had written "Interesting Answer."

Goober sidled closer and looked over my shoulder, practically digging his chin into it.

"A," he said reverently. "You got an A." He opened his own envelope and I had no qualms about looking over *his* shoulder.

He'd got a C, and Mr. Castor had written, "I

don't quite understand the references to weird foreigners employing their leisure moments to seize heights. Just as confusing to me is the sentence about weighing our neighbors. Please clarify."

Goober sighed. "I'll have to practice my memory aids more often," he said.

10 · Standing on My Head Would Have Been Better

If I wasn't a real Fairlee Boy by now, I never would be. I'd been to about a million classes, I'd tried a hundred times to learn how to shoot arrows, and I'd been on plenty of bird walks. It had turned out that you couldn't watch birds from your dormitory window—you had to go out in the woods, and to get out in the woods you had to get out of bed.

The most important thing was that I'd watched all of the banana programs but two. Of course, I'd had to come up with some more excuses for Mrs. Pomeroy. The last time, I'd told her I couldn't be in class because a writer was

coming to interview me for a series of articles he
was doing about education in private schools.
She'd looked at me a little strangely but relaxed
when I explained that the journalist in question
was a very, very good friend of my parents and
it was a high honor for me and, of course, for
Fairlee to have been chosen.

The commercials had been getting harder to
follow. The commercial of the last show (with
those banana puppets singing) had gone like this:

Nannabee, nannabee, banna-bee-ban
Nannabee, bannabee, bananabee-nan!

Two bananas, but it sounded like more, unless
you really paid attention. You had to be a pretty
expert commercial-watcher to succeed at this
kind of thing, and I was glad I'd spent so much
of my life getting to be good at it. It was just the
way Goober had always said: You never know
when a certain skill will come in handy.

The next "Banana Blitz" show was coming up
next Wednesday. I didn't even know if I'd live
that long: I hadn't had a candy bar for days and
was suffering pangs that were probably going to
prove fatal. Dad's check should have come before now. I'd looked in my mail slot every single

day, and so far all the mail I'd had was a series of interschool memos.

After lunch Friday I looked again. And there it was, finally: an envelope from Dad. I tore it open. A folded check inside. Probably fifty dollars. Maybe more.

Good old Dad. I knew I could count on him, especially after my great letter. I'd buy a batch of candy bars right away.

I unfolded the check and stared at it. Five dollars! *Five!* That wouldn't last me a week.

I opened his letter and skimmed through it quickly. ". . . the school provides . . . we have spent . . . watch your expenses carefully . . . hope this check will obviate the necessity for further interim financing."

I read it again: ". . . obviate the necessity for further interim financing." What was *that* supposed to mean? I read it once more. Fortunately, living with Goober had enabled me to translate just about any meaningless sentence, so I was finally able to decipher this one. What it meant was: I hope you won't need any more money.

I sighed one of my better sighs and tried to visualize my existence without candy bars. It was like looking at the end of my life.

Banana Bingo was my only prayer now.

That next Wednesday, Mr. Castor gave us a geography quiz. "Just a miniquiz," he assured us. "Just to keep you on your toes, so to speak."

One of the questions was: Name the Great Lakes.

HOMES, I muttered to myself, putting the letters in a column:

H
O
M
E
S

I finally got them all:

HURON
ONTARIO
MICHIGAN
ERIE
SUPERIOR

At least I'd get one of the quiz questions right.

After we'd handed our papers in, Goober sidled up to me.

"I couldn't remember my poem," he whined. "So I couldn't think of all the Great Lakes. Just Ontario, because I knew it had to rhyme with *there-ee-oh*. What's the Great Lake that begins with *U?* Maybe I've been studying too much."

"There isn't one that begins with *U,*" I told him.

"Of course there is," said Goober. "I'm positive of that because of my memory device. *HOUSE.*"

"Homes, not house," I said graciously.

"Oh. Well, I was close." Goober sighed.

"Sure, you were," I said, edging away. I could afford to be gracious.

Now I had to get to Mrs. Pomeroy's class—fast.

I ran down the hall until I came to the washroom. Good. I was the only one there.

I turned on the hot water and let it run. While I was waiting for it to get really hot, I put my head between my legs to get the blood to my face so I'd look flushed. Standing on my head would have been better, of course, but a lot more work.

I tested the water: hot. I ducked my face under it for a couple of minutes.

By the time I got to Mrs. Pomeroy's room, my

face was as red and as hot as I could make it. I walked over to her desk.

"I don't know what's the matter with me, Mrs. Pomeroy, but I've got this terrible headache and sore throat, and I think I probably have a very high temperature as well."

She was busy writing and didn't look up right away. "Just a second," she murmured.

I couldn't afford to wait even a minute, because I was cooling off fast, so I sort of slumped over and said, "I think I'm going to faint or something, I'm so dizzy."

She looked up, alarmed. "Goodness gracious, Jonah," she said. "You look very flushed." She put her hand on my head. "I do believe you have a fever," she decided.

"That's just what I was afraid of," I told her. "And I especially wanted to be in class this afternoon. I hate to miss even one period. But I'm afraid I have no choice." I held my head. "I'm very disappointed, as I say, to miss your stimulating class, but I'll just have to go back to my room and lie down."

Mrs. Pomeroy stood up purposefully. "We'll have to put you in the infirmary," she said.

The infirmary!

"Come with me to the office," she said. "I'll call Nurse Appleton, and . . ."

My plan had boomeranged. Now what? I glanced at the big clock on the wall. I had fifteen minutes to get over to the dorm and the television set. I couldn't possibly go to the infirmary. I'd miss the program. My life would be over.

Mrs. Pomeroy started out of the room. "Come along, Jonah," she said.

I thought quickly. If I pretended that I had suddenly recovered, I'd be stuck in Mrs. Pomeroy's class. I'd miss the program. And then I'd die.

"Mrs. Pomeroy, I'm afraid I won't be able to go to the infirmary," I told her. "It's something that I don't like to talk about. My parents urged me to put this into my answers in the questionnaire this summer, but the fact is I was ashamed to have the school know of my problem." I hung my head. "I should have listened to my parents," I said with a very convincing sigh.

Mrs. Pomeroy turned around. "You didn't want the school to know what?" she demanded.

What indeed, I wondered. "Well," I said, stalling for time, waiting until an idea would wander into my brain, "it's an inherited characteristic.

My father has it, and his father before him, who was of course my grandfather. And *his* father," I added. "He was my great-grandfather."

"Yes?" asked Mrs. Pomeroy. "Get on with it, Jonah."

"It's a rare affliction," I went on. "An unusual disorder. It is not dangerous, it is not contagious. It's just . . . unusual." I could tell she was getting impatient. In another second she'd drag me off to the infirmary, so I hurried on.

"It's just that when we have these spells, we have to lie down. In familiar surroundings. Hospital beds, infirmaries, simply aggravate the condition. And that would indeed prove to be dangerous to our health. Not to my great-grandfather's health, you understand. It's too late for him now. He's . . . no longer living." I swallowed. "I should have informed the school before I arrived," I went on. "But I was afraid that Fairlee wouldn't accept me, and I'd really always wanted to be a Fairlee Boy."

Her eyes misted over. Well, they didn't exactly mist over—I think she was about to sneeze, or maybe yawn, in fact, but I decided I was on the right track.

"Admittedly, it is a strange thing," I said. "A

medical curiosity. But I assure you that if I can just go back to my familiar bed in the dorm, close my eyes for an hour or so, this episode will pass. If, however, I were to be sent to the infirmary, I don't know what would happen. I've told you about my great-grandfather and the fact that he is no longer among the living. And the reason for that is—"

"Very well," said Mrs. Pomeroy, looking at me suspiciously. "You may be excused." I hurried out of her room before she could change her mind, and headed back to the dorm and the next program.

It was a tough series of commercials, but I wrote down on the Banana Bingo chart every single mention of the word *banana*. I was one program closer to my five hundred dollars.

That night we had Fruit Delight. We were each served something that looked sort of like a banana split but wasn't. Instead of ice cream and stuff on top of the banana (which was split the long way, as in a banana split), there were two mounds of cottage cheese colored with food coloring (one pink mound, one green), and a maraschino cherry on top of each one. Over all that were apple slices and sections of oranges and grapefruit and some canned fruit cocktail.

My mother would have been proud of Sammie.

Everyone at the table was grumbling. "What's this supposed to be, a big bowl of vitamins?" and "Holy banana!" and "I should have stayed in bed!"

Sammie, in a white outfit of some kind and a white chef's hat, was walking in my direction. If he'd been wearing a surgical mask, he'd have looked like a doctor or a nurse or one of those fathers who participate in having babies.

I hoped the kids at my table wouldn't say anything about the Fruit Delight. Most of them had scraped everything off the bananas and were eating the bananas. "How was it?" Sammie asked anxiously, leaning over to whisper in my ear.

"Great," I lied. "Terrific. Good way to use up bananas."

"Did you get down all the bananas?" he asked.

At first I thought he was asking if I'd been able to swallow the Fruit Delight, but then I realized he was talking about the banana commercials. "I got them all down, they're all on the chart, it was a snap," I said proudly.

"I'm very, *very* glad to hear that," he said. "I've been thinking about it all day."

"Don't worry," I bragged. "I've got everything under control."

As soon as he had wandered back to the kitchen, I scraped off all the cottage cheese and stuff and ate *my* banana. Actually, I was getting pretty tired of bananas. I hoped Sammie would use them all up pretty soon.

11 · Yes, We Have No Bananas

Brrrrrrrrrring! Brrrrrrrrrring!

What was that bell, and why was it ringing in the middle of the night?

I sat up in bed and tried to get awake. Maybe it was a fire drill or something.

I stumbled out of bed, reached for my lamp, knocked it over, stubbed my toe, and finally found the light switch.

It was Goober's alarm clock that was ringing. It was one o'clock. I stalked over to his bed, shut off the alarm, and shook him awake.

"You idiot, why did you set your alarm to go off in the middle of the night?" I yelled.

Goober yawned and looked at the clock. He

had that white ointment on his face and that stocking thing on his hair, and his yawn wasn't very attractive.

He stretched and got out of bed.

"I read an article on sleep," Goober explained. "It said that the most beneficial sleep you get is during those first three hours."

"And?" I asked threateningly.

"And so I figured that if the first three hours are the best, then I'd sleep three hours, be awake for a while, and then get another very beneficial three hours, and so on. So I'm testing it out. I'll keep reaping all the benefits of those first three hours of sleep, see? And so will you. As I've told you, I am willing to share with you the benefits of my research."

He picked up his alarm clock and reset it. "It's one o'clock now," he said. "We've both had the maximum benefit of our important first three hours of sleep. Now we just go back to sleep, wake up at four o'clock, and we'll have had another three very, very good hours of beneficial sleep."

He adjusted his stocking cap and reached for the jar of white ointment.

"I may be onto a real breakthrough in this

field. I'm thinking of writing an article about it."

"And I'm thinking of writing an article about you," I said dangerously.

"That would be a bit premature," he said. "But I'm gratified that you recognize in me an original talent. Actually, because you have an opportunity to observe me closely and under all circumstances and conditions, at all times of day and night, you are in a unique position to write a definitive biography of me when the time comes. When you think of it that way, it's a very, very fortunate thing for you that you have this exposure to me at this critical time in my development."

"You bet it's a critical time in your development," I said, stalking across the room and grabbing the alarm clock. "If I hear one more sound out of this clock, your budding career will be nipped in the bud."

"You should have an open mind," whined Goober. "You don't give my ideas a chance. If you try this new sleeping program for a few nights, you'll find that you have extra vitality, additional vigor. We're roommates. We should share our ideas and our experiences with each other."

I stuffed the alarm clock in my bureau drawer.

It was either that or throwing it and Goober out of the window, which would have been a noisier but a more satisfying experience.

"Look," I said. "I don't want to share every single thing with you. I don't want your advice on everything, about how or whether I should breathe. All I want is my half of the room, my half of the closet, my half of the refrigerator, and my half of the television set. I don't want to see or hear you or your clock or your sardines. I want to sleep."

"I don't think you have the right spirit," said Goober, snuffling. "I don't think you get the idea of what having a roommate is all about."

"I get the idea, all right," I said. "You get your half, I get my half. That's all there is to it."

"Taking my alarm clock is an invasion of privacy," whined Goober. "You have no right to appropriate any possessions of mine. I could report you."

"Report away!" I urged him. "Take it to the Supreme Court."

I finally went back to sleep, listening to Goober's sighs.

Brrrrrriinnnng!
I struggled to get awake. It couldn't be the

alarm clock, so it must be the Fairlee wake-up bell. Goober was snoring softly. I stumbled out of bed, started across the room, tripped, and fell, banging my head, shins, elbows, and knees extremely hard. I could see that what I'd tripped on was a clothesline that was stretched across the room at ankle level.

"You shouldn't scream like that," said Goober reprovingly, sitting up in bed. "It's upsetting to wake up that way. That was very inconsiderate of you."

I sat up, felt to see whether I had any broken bones, and glared at Goober.

"What is this?" I asked angrily. "You're trying to kill me."

Goober adjusted his stocking cap and looked at the clothesline. "Oh, that. Well, you kept complaining about dividing the room equally, so after you went back to sleep I measured it off. That clothesline divides the room into two equal parts. As you will notice, we each have half of the window and the window ledge, half of the refrigerator, and half of the TV set. I really worked very hard to make it absolutely fair."

I started to grit my teeth but realized I'd banged my jaw on the way down, and it hurt.

"You're very hard to please." Goober sighed.

"There's nothing I can do to satisfy you. You wanted the room divided in half, so I divided it in half. Now you're complaining again. Your problem is that you've never had to share anything before now, since you haven't any siblings. It's taking you an unusually long time to adjust to the idea of living with a roommate and sharing."

"I have news for you," I said. "I will never adjust. And the only way I can survive the unusual experience of sharing a room with you is not to hear another word from you."

"You'll discover—" Goober started to say.

"Not one word, now or later or ever," I warned him.

Goober sighed one of his tragic sighs. "You'll change your mind after a few days," he said. "You're just overtired."

I stood up painfully and walked over to the bathroom. A shower would help get me awake. The bathtub was filled, of course, with every towel we owned, all covered with fish oil, zinc oxide ointment, and sardine juice.

It had been a really busy week. I hadn't even had a chance to read the new *TV Guide.* The best thing about the week was that Goober wasn't talking. He was sighing a lot, but he wasn't talking.

Today was the last "Banana Blitz" program. The last of the commercials. I'd be able to finish filling in the Banana Bingo card, and then I'd get my share of the thousand-dollar prize. Life was going to change very rapidly. Five hundred dollars!

I was sure Mrs. Pomeroy was beginning to get suspicious of all my excuses, so I decided to skip her class altogether today. I'd tell her tomorrow that I'd become very, *very* sick and had had to go back to my room to *be* sick.

I had lots of time before the banana program would begin. I walked slowly across the empty campus. Everyone else but me was in class. Actually, Fairlee wouldn't be a bad place to live if it weren't for having to go to classes. And having Goober for a roommate.

When I walked into Room 22, I heard a lot of splashing around in the bathroom, and in a minute a dripping Goober opened the bathroom door. What a jolt! I didn't want him around while I was trying to watch the banana commercials.

"What are you doing here?" I demanded. "You're supposed to be in class." I'd forgotten, for the moment, that Goober and I weren't talking.

"I knew you'd change your mind about not talking," he said. "Actually, I've been skipping classes for the past few days. I'm re-examining some of my priorities. I'm trying to get an objective look at my habits and my goals. Sometimes we have to step aside, intellectually, and observe ourselves as others might see us."

I'd forgotten how blissful the last few days had been without his incessant jabbering.

"I felt I needed a change of pace," he went on. "All work and no play makes Jack a dull boy. The name Jack, of course, in this instance, means anyone, of whatever name. It's just an expression, you understand."

"I understand," I told him. "I also understand, and hope for your sake that you do, that there is to be no conversation. I'm watching my banana program and I need complete silence."

"But—" Goober whined.

"Complete, utter, and total silence," I said.

He shook his head sadly and started back into the bathroom. "One of the things I'm experimenting with today is a twenty-four-hour period with a new ointment."

He closed the bathroom door just in the nick of time.

I flicked on the television set. I still had a few minutes before the banana program was scheduled. I sat on my bed and picked up the *TV Guide*, stretched happily, and started to read. There were lots of good shows coming up, including a made-for-TV movie that looked great.

Suddenly a paragraph caught my eye:

DUE TO CIRCUMSTANCES BEYOND OUR CONTROL THE SIXTH AND FINAL "BANANA BLITZ" PROGRAM SPONSORED BY THE AMERICAN BANANA INSTITUTE HAS BEEN SCHEDULED THREE DAYS EARLIER THAN PLANNED AND WILL BE AIRED ON MONDAY, OCTOBER 15, INSTEAD OF WEDNESDAY, OCTOBER 17. WE APOLOGIZE FOR ANY INCONVENIENCE THIS MAY HAVE CAUSED OUR VIEWERS.

I read it again. Then I stared at it stupidly. Then I stared into space. The banana show was already over! They'd run it on Monday! I'd missed the banana commercials and the chance of winning the thousand dollars for Sammie and me.

What I'd do now, I couldn't imagine. Drown myself in the bathtub, probably.

I closed my eyes and lay back on the bed. All the banana commercials rang in my head. Bananabee-ban, nannabee-nan. This had to be the worst time in my entire life. I'd missed the show. Yes, we have no bananas. Yes, we have no thousand dollars.

There was a knock at the door, and I dragged myself out of bed. Maybe I'd fallen asleep and was dreaming, because a huge banana stood in the hall.

"Jonah D. Krock?" asked the banana. It was someone in a banana costume, like some of those people on the American Banana Institute commercials.

"I have a singing telegram for you," said the banana. "And then, of course, you will be presented with your banana bonus. And, of course, your check." The banana started to sing:

> *Congratulations to you,*
> *Congratulations to you,*
> *Congratulations, dear contest winner,*
> *Congratulations to you!*

I kept staring at the banana.

"And if you'll just sign here, please, we'll bring up your banana bonus. It's in the lobby. Had to be sure you were here."

He held out a receipt for me to sign, and I signed it. I'd sort of forgotten my name or how the signature was supposed to go, but I finally managed.

"I'll be right back," said the banana. "Congratulations." He looked at the name plate on the door. "Congratulations, Fish," he added.

I was still standing there when Goober came out of the bathroom. I could hear him snuffling and slurping around, reciting something under his breath. It sounded like "Fee fi fo fum," but it probably wasn't.

"A banana was just here," I said.

Goober eyed me suspiciously.

"That's very nice," he said in a soothing voice. "The fact is that you have always had a curious fondness for bananas, and now, after weeks of academic stress and the difficult adjustment of living away from home, it is only natural that bananas play a role in your dreams. Or it may be that you have experienced a hallucination. That is rare, of course, but not impossible. You may not be eating a balanced diet. Occasionally junk food in quantity alters our perceptions of reality, and—"

The banana had appeared at the door again.

This time there were a couple of people with him. Delivery men. Delivery men with bunches and bunches of bananas.

"Where do you want them?" the banana asked cheerfully.

Goober came up behind me. I couldn't talk. "I guess you'll have to put them in the bathtub," he said.

The delivery men filled the tub with the bananas and stacked the rest of them on the bathroom floor and on the floor of our room.

"So much for the banana bonus," said the banana. "And now, of course, here's your check. Congratulations!" And he was gone.

"I think you're right, about my hallucinating," I finally said to Goober. "Maybe I *should* have something to eat. Is there anything in the refrigerator? A big cake of yeast or some leftover sardines or something?"

"Bananas, as you probably know, are a good source of potassium" he said. He stepped over some of the bunches of bananas and opened the refrigerator door. "But you may prefer a candy bar for quick energy." He took out a candy bar and handed it to me. "I bought a lot, the other day," he said. "It was all part of my program of looking at things in a new way."

I sat down on my bed, holding the candy bar in one hand and the envelope that the banana had given me in the other. I didn't have enough strength to open either one.

"Of course, as we both now realize," said Goober, "the banana was not a hallucination after all. It was simply a representative of the American Banana Institute, dressed up to resemble a large banana."

He reached into his desk drawer and took out a jar of cream, opened it, and applied some to his chin.

"I told you I've been skipping classes. I wanted to think things over, arrange my priorities. I realized that although I had always urged you to have an open mind, I had not always had one. I had tried to impose my beliefs on you without giving yours a chance."

I looked away from Goober and started to look at the envelope. "Jonah D. Krock," it said. That was me. I was pretty sure it was, anyway.

"For example," said Goober, "I had regarded television viewing as a poor habit, unless, of course, the program in question was an educational one. I had scoffed at your insistence on watching game shows. I couldn't comprehend the fact that you even watched commercials. Well, last Monday, all that changed. I decided to try your way, just for one day. After all, an open mind is a growing mind."

I was still in a daze. I hadn't even opened the envelope.

"I turned on television, and that banana program was on."

He set the jar of cream down and walked over to my desk.

"Actually, the entire experience has proved to me that my original premise was correct, and that premise is, as you will recall, an open mind is a growing mind."

My own mind had gone into reverse.

"I found it, surprisingly, quite a challenge to keep track of all the occasions the word *banana* was used in the commercials. It really kept me on my toes, although that is, of course, just a figure of speech. Actually I was, as I have said, sitting on the bed and was not, therefore, on my toes."

He handed me the Banana Bingo chart. I tried to get my mind in gear.

"As I believe you have already discovered—

after all, you won the contest—I kept an accurate score. I am, as you may have observed, a perfectionist."

My mind swam slowly into focus. Goober had watched that last banana show, had listened for all the times the word *banana* had been used in the commercials, had marked it down on the chart. I looked at the Banana Bingo chart. It was all filled in.

"Of course, this is a Xerox copy of the original. I took the original chart down to the supermarket." Goober stepped over the piles of bananas to his own bed. He sat down and continued to rub the cream on his face.

"I am happy that you have the satisfaction of winning as well as the tangible reward of a large check. As for me, it is reward enough to have proved my point: An open mind is the sign of an educated man."

I felt like hugging him—sardines, fish oil, stocking cap, and all. I resisted the impulse.

"By the way," he said, "this new cream really seems to work."

"I see a big improvement," I lied.

I opened the envelope. One thousand dollars. I could hardly wait to tell Sammie.

And I could hardly wait to put in that supply of candy bars and stuff.

"Goober, you are really something. I mean: you are really *some*thing."

I'd said that before, but it hadn't meant the same thing.

After all, it's not what you say, it's how you say it.

ABOUT THE AUTHOR

FLORENCE PARRY HEIDE is the author of many books for young readers, including *The Shrinking of Treehorn, Treehorn's Treasure*, and *Banana Twist* (all A.L.A. Notable Books). *Banana Twist*, a companion to this volume, "is brimming with zany characters and hilarious situations" *(Horn Book)* and is "told with sparkling ease . . . ooz[ing] funny situations at every turn of the page" *(Booklist)*. It has also been nominated for five state awards and was a winner of the Charlie Mae Simon Award in Arkansas.

A native of Pittsburgh, Pennsylvania, and a graduate of the University of California at Los Angeles, Mrs. Heide lives in Kenosha, Wisconsin. She is married to an attorney, Donald Heide, and they have five children and three grandchildren.